Also by Heather Grovet

Ready to Ride Series
A Perfect Star

Zippitty Do Dah

More titles coming!

Other books by Heather Grovet
Beanie: The Horse That Wasn't a Horse

Marvelous Mark and His No-good Dog

Petunia the Ugly Pug

Prince: The Persnickety Pony That Didn't Like Grown-ups

Prince Prances Again

Sarah Lee and a Mule Named Maybe

What's Wrong With Rusty?

GOOD AS GOLD

Heather Grovet Series Book Three

READY TO RIDE SERIES

Pacific Press® Publishing Association
Nampa, Idaho
Oshawa, Ontario, Canada
www.pacificpress.com

Book design by Gerald Lee Monks
Cover photo/illustration © Mary Bausman

Additional copies of this book are available by calling
toll-free 1-800-765-6955 or by
visiting http://www.adventistbookcenter.com.

Library of Congress Cataloging-in-Publication Data

Grovet, Heather, 1963-
Good as gold : discovering what is really important /
Heather Grovet.
p. cm. — (Ready to ride ; bk. 3)
Summary: When friends Kendra, Ruth-Ann, and
Megan enter horseback riding competitions, they soon
discover that they must trust God to show them what
is really important.
ISBN 13: 978-0-8163-2166-7
ISBN 10: 0–8163–2166-3
[1. Ponies. 2. Friendship. 3. Christian life.] I. Title.

PZ7.G931825Goo 2007
dc22   2006052784

07 08 09 10 11 • 5 4 3 2 1

Dedication

To my Morgan friends, Cindy and Lyle Dietz, who always challenge me and my Paints at local horse shows!

Contents

Blondie Jumps

"Today's the day!" Trish, the riding instructor, told ten-year-old Megan Lewis. "Blondie's going to do her first real jumping course. And I want you to do it from start to finish without stopping."

Megan nervously tightened the buckle to her riding helmet and patted the neck of her Palomino pony, Blondie. "OK," she said. "I won't stop. Unless I fall off, of course!"

"You won't fall off," Trish said. "You've got a good teacher helping you. Right? Now, there are six jumps set in an S-shaped pattern." She pointed to the jumps in order, showing Megan where she should turn. "Got it?"

"I hope so," Megan said. Blondie held her head high, and her golden ears swiveled back and forth as she studied the jumps eagerly, almost as though she were trying to memorize their order! Megan smiled in spite of her nervousness. Blondie seemed to enjoy jumping as much as she did, but it would be up to Megan to tell her which direction to go.

"I'll probably get lost," Megan said.

"How do you get lost in a riding ring?" Trish asked.

"I don't mean I'll get *lost*," Megan said. "I mean I'll forget which order to do the jumps in."

"Then stop and ask me," Trish said.

"I thought you said I shouldn't stop," Megan said.

Trish rolled her eyes. "Just do the best you can," she said.

"OK," Megan said. "Wish me luck."

"Break a leg," Trish said.

"Break a leg?" Megan exclaimed.

Trish laughed. "Sorry," she said. "That's probably a poor expression for a horse rider!

But you know what I mean. And I really don't believe in luck, anyhow. I'd rather trust God than luck."

"I know," Megan said. "Me too." She tightened her grip on the reins and pushed Blondie into an energetic trot. *We can do this,* she told herself. Megan squeezed her legs and cantered the Palomino pony toward the first jump.

Blondie didn't hesitate. She galloped to the first jump, her ears pricked forward, and sprang effortlessly over it. In a few more strides she was at a tall blue jump, which she also easily cleared.

One jump after another disappeared under Blondie as she circled the arena, following Megan's directions. When Blondie landed the last jump, Megan leaned back in the saddle and used her arms and shoulders to bring Blondie into a smooth turn to the left.

Megan's two best friends, Kendra Rawling and Ruth-Ann Chow, were sitting outside the riding ring on their ponies, Star and Zipper. They clapped their hands wildly, and

Kendra even managed a wobbly wolf whistle. Megan grinned as she sat deeply in her saddle and applied steady pressure to both reins. Blondie cantered ahead a few more strides and then broke into a brisk trot. The pair made a small circle at the far end of the riding ring and then came to a halt.

"There," Trish called. "That wasn't so difficult, was it?"

"I was scared to death!" Megan said. "But we did it, anyhow."

"You did a great job," Kendra called.

"Super-duper job!" Ruth-Ann shouted.

"Well," Megan said with a satisfied feeling. "It must have been OK because I didn't get lost. And I didn't fall off either."

"Blondie jumps like a kangaroo," Ruth-Ann said.

"A kangaroo!" Megan exclaimed. "Is that good or bad?"

"It's good, of course," Ruth-Ann said.

"Raise the jumps!" Kendra suggested. "Blondie can jump much higher!"

Trish shook her head. "That's enough for

today," she said. "We want Blondie to enjoy jumping!"

"Enjoy jumping?" Kendra said. "Blondie loves jumping!"

"I love jumping too," Megan said. She flung her arms around the Palomino's amber neck and squeezed tight. "And I love Blondie even more."

"Let's end on a good note," Trish said. "While everyone's so happy and lovable!" She called the other girls into the ring.

Megan watched her friends ride toward her. In the lead was Kendra, riding her white Welsh pony, Star. Star was the smallest of the ponies, standing about 13 hands high, and she was beautiful, with a delicate dished face and long flowing mane and tail.

Ruth-Ann followed at a slower pace on Zipper. Zipper wasn't actually a pony, but instead a small Paint horse about 14.2 hands high. He was a coppery sorrel color with large zigzaggy patches of white all over him. Even Zipper's mane was part white and part brown.

Megan looked down at Blondie and

smiled. Blondie was the middle-sized pony. She was bigger and heavier than Star, but shorter than Zipper. Blondie was half Morgan and half Welsh, and had a proud, upright neck and thick creamy mane almost the same color as Megan's own blond hair.

The three girls had been taking riding lessons with Trish all summer, and Megan could hardly believe how much Blondie had improved. Only a few months earlier Blondie had been strong-willed and stubborn. She had turned when she wanted to, but not necessarily when Megan wanted her to. She stopped when she wanted, and she started when it suited her too. Now things were different.

Everything had changed when Kendra, Ruth-Ann, and Megan started a riding club called Ready to Ride, or R2R for short. They worked together to solve horse problems, and one of the things they had done was find a horse trainer to help Kendra teach Star to jump. That trainer was Trish. Megan knew that Blondie would not have improved without Trish's help and a lot of hard work on her part.

Ready to Show?

Trish spoke, interrupting Megan's thoughts. "You girls have made a lot of progress this month," she said. "I can tell you're practicing faithfully."

"The R2R members ride every day," Megan said. "Unless it rains."

"Or snows," Kendra added.

"And strangely enough, it hasn't snowed all summer," Ruth-Ann said. "So we've had to keep practicing!"

"We don't practice our riding lessons on Sabbath," Ruth-Ann said. "But we trail ride for fun. Last Saturday afternoon we rode all the way to town and back."

"That's a long trip," Trish said. "You must have been tired when you were finished."

"We had a picnic supper at the half-way point," Megan said. "It was so much fun. Mrs. Rawling sent cheese buns, and my mom made fresh fruit salad."

"Someone forgot the spoons," Kendra said. "So it was rather tricky eating the fruit salad."

"Sorry," Megan said, shrugging.

"I brought the dessert," Ruth-Ann giggled. "It was candy from my little brother's birthday party! But we didn't get to eat it. While we were hunting for the spoons, Zipper got into the bag and ate the candy when we weren't looking."

"Zipper ate a whole bag of candy?" Trish asked.

"Not a *whole* bag," Ruth-Ann said. "He left the chocolate-covered peanuts."

Kendra groaned. "The peanuts were covered with gross horse slobber, so we had to throw them away!"

"You girls always have so much fun with your Ready to Ride Club," Trish said. "I'd have loved a club like that when I was a kid."

"It was my mom's idea," Kendra said. "She had a club with my Aunt Connie and some other girls called The Happy Riders. They had lots of fun and adventures."

"Well, thanks to your club's riding practices and lessons, your ponies are becoming very well trained," Trish said. "And your own riding positions are excellent."

The three girls looked at each other. No one said anything for a moment, but they knew what the others were thinking.

"Do you think . . ." Megan asked slowly, looking at Trish. "Do you think that . . ."

"Would we be ready . . ." Kendra asked.

"Is there any chance . . ." Ruth-Ann continued.

"Could we possibly . . ."

Trish broke into laughter. "OK," she said. "The R2R Club must be better horse riders than talkers, because I have absolutely no idea what you're asking me!"

"There's a horse show at the end of August," Megan said.

"A *real* horse show," Kendra added.

"At the Hastings Lake Fairgrounds," Megan continued. "They're going to have a real judge, and real ribbons."

"There are classes for adults and kids of all ages," Ruth-Ann said. "Walk/trot classes for the beginners, and more difficult classes for the experienced riders."

"The show's on a Thursday," Kendra said. "So we could go."

"If we're ready," Ruth-Ann said.

"Do you think we'll be ready?" Megan asked.

"Ready for what?" Trish asked. A faint smile curved the corners of her mouth.

"Will we be ready to show?" the three girls shouted together.

Trish smiled. "Well, of course you'll be ready to show," she said.

"We will?"

"You'll be ready to show," Trish said. "But maybe not ready to win."

The girls looked at Trish and then back at each other. "Oh," they said.

"Maybe you will be ready to win," Trish continued, "but maybe not, either. And showing isn't about winning, anyhow."

"I'd like to win," Megan said.

"Me too," Kendra agreed.

"Me three," Ruth-Ann said quickly.

"Everyone would like to win," Trish said. "But that isn't the main reason for going to horse shows."

"It isn't?" Ruth-Ann asked.

"A ribbon isn't worth very much," Trish said. "You can go to any trophy shop and buy a ribbon for a dollar or two. Horse shows aren't about ribbons; they're about improving your and your horse's abilities. If you have a good attitude and ask God to bless you and keep you safe, you can have fun even if you don't win any ribbons."

"I'll need God to help me with my attitude," Megan said. "Because I'd like to win a ribbon just once. I've been to shows with my family before, but I never did very well."

"God's an expert on good attitudes," Trish said. "If you ask Him, He'll help."

Megan nodded.

"We can enter Western classes," Ruth-Ann said. "Since we all have Western tack."

"Could we enter English classes too?" Kendra asked.

"Maybe I could borrow a couple of English saddles for Megan and Ruth-Ann," Trish replied.

"That would be great," Kendra said. "Could Star and I enter the jumping classes?"

She pushed her long brown hair out of her face.

Trish thought for a moment. "I don't think Star is ready for an actual jumping class," she said. "Jumping classes are timed, and you'd have to rush Star over a big course. I don't think she's ready for that. But you could enter hunter hack."

"Hunter hack?" Kendra asked.

"Hunter hack isn't timed," Trish said. "You're judged on your horse's ability to look pretty when going over two low jumps. That would be a good start for Star's jumping classes."

"OK," Kendra said.

"I won't enter any jumping classes," Ruth-Ann said. "Zipper isn't ready. But I'd like to enter some regular classes on the flat, both English and Western. If I could borrow an English saddle."

Megan loosened her riding helmet's chin strap thoughtfully. Jumping was so important to her that she almost hated to ask Trish if she thought Blondie was ready to compete. But Trish seemed to know what Megan was thinking, because she turned to the girl before she could ask anything.

"Now Blondie's a different kettle of fish altogether," Trish said.

"Blondie isn't even a fish," Megan said with a grin. "She's a pony, Trish!"

"Blondie's a different ball of wax," the woman said. "I think she's ready for a low jumper class. Blondie is very confident when she jumps. And she can turn sharply and get into position very easily. Jumping comes naturally to her."

Megan's face flushed pink underneath her thick blond hair. "Really?" she asked. "Do you mean it, Trish?"

"Have I ever lied to you before?" Trish asked.

Blondie picked that minute to bob her head up and down. It looked almost as though she was saying that Trish had, in fact, lied to them before! Everyone laughed.

After Trish left, the three girls unsaddled and then brushed their ponies' sweaty backs. "This is going to be so much fun," Megan said, standing back to admire Blondie's gleaming gold coat. "We can enter a real horse show together."

"The other riders better watch out!" Kendra said.

Ruth-Ann nodded her head in agreement. "The Ready to Ride Club is going to knock their socks off!"

"We'll do better than that!" Megan said.

"We're going to knock their socks *and* their riding boots off!"

"I'm going to win a first-place ribbon," Kendra said. She brushed Star so firmly that little fluffs of white hair flew through the air.

"I'm going to win a first-place ribbon too," Ruth-Ann said. "Maybe two."

Megan looked at her friends. For once they were too busy with their ponies to notice the expression on her face.

Megan had shown horses before with her mother and older sister, Mandy. She knew that horse shows could be very difficult. There were always a lot of well-trained horses and experienced riders.

And Blondie had a mind of her own. Sometimes she was as good as gold. That was Blondie's registered name—Good as Gold Blondie. But sometimes Blondie wasn't so good. Sometimes she was a big, blond brat! Thanks to Trish the bratty times happened less often now, but Megan knew they could happen again, especially during a noisy and exciting event like a horse show.

And everyone wanted to win a first-place ribbon.

What would happen when the R2R girls competed against each other? Only one person could win first place. Would that make the other girls angry?

Megan sighed and reached for a hoof pick. She had never really enjoyed showing horses before. Showing at Hastings Lake with her friends sounded like fun, but Megan also imagined it could cause problems.

The Ready to Ride Club would never let ribbons be more important than their friendship. Would they?

Megan thought she'd need to talk to God about that. He would have to help the whole R2R Club. He would have to help her with her attitude too, because right then Megan could close her eyes and picture a handful of brightly colored rosettes. And they all belonged to her and Blondie—Good as Gold Blondie.

Bareback Riding

A few days later the girls and their ponies met at the Lewis farm. Megan's family had a wonderful arena where the R2R club often rode. The arena was large, with smooth, sandy footing, and it had a white wooden rail around the outside. There were dozens of fun obstacles to do with the ponies if they grew tired of practicing their basic walk, trot, and canter. There was a wooden bridge to walk over, a swinging metal gate to open and close, and tires, pylons, and poles to set in various patterns.

Megan had suggested they ride bareback that afternoon, but the other two weren't so certain. "Trish said riding bareback would be a good way to improve our balance," Megan told the others encouragingly. She slipped the snaffle bit into Blondie mouth and then pulled the bridle's brow band over the pony's ears. "And it's so easy to get ready. We don't have to blanket and saddle or anything. We just hop on and go!"

"I don't know," Kendra said. "Sometimes I ride Star at home bareback, but we aren't very good. And we only ride at a walk; otherwise I think I'd tip off!"

"I don't normally ride bareback either," Megan said. "But we could all try together."

"Just thinking about riding without a saddle makes me nervous," Ruth-Ann admitted.

"Zipper won't run away or buck," Megan said. "He's always so well behaved."

"Zipper will be OK," Ruth-Ann said, gazing up at Zipper's back, which seemed to tower above her. "But will I be OK? He's awfully tall, and I know I'll fall off a few times."

"You won't fall off," Megan said. "And the arena ground is really soft, anyhow."

"And you have your new riding helmet," Kendra said. "So you won't be hurt."

"Are you going to ride bareback?" Ruth-Ann asked Kendra.

Kendra pursed her lips and thought. Finally she nodded her head. "I guess so," she said. "I can always saddle Star later if I want."

"I've never ridden bareback before," Ruth-Ann said. "Not even once."

"I've ridden bareback a few times," Kendra said. "Mostly when I catch Star at the far end of the pasture and I don't want to walk home in my cowboy boots! And look what I learned to do."

Kendra put the reins over Star's neck and took a handful of the pony's long white mane in both hands. She took a deep breath and then jumped up onto Star's shoulders. Kendra wiggled her feet once or twice and swung onto Star's back with a pleased grin.

Megan clapped her hands. "You look like a real cowgirl," she said.

"And Star didn't move a muscle!" Ruth-Ann said.

"That's how I mount in the pasture," Kendra said. "I have to get on without help."

"I'll never get on Zipper without stairs or an elevator!" Ruth-Ann moaned. She reached up and copied Kendra by grabbing hold of Zipper's mane and jumping, but no matter how hard she tried, she couldn't get even halfway into position.

"Zipper's a lot taller than Star," Megan said. "Here, let me give you a boost." In a moment Ruth-Ann was perched on Zipper's sorrel-and-white back.

"How does it feel?" Kendra asked.

"I never realized how boney Zipper's back is," Ruth-Ann said. She wiggled around a little and then smiled at the other girls. "But I think we'll be OK!"

"Now it's my turn," Megan said. She looked at Blondie, who was standing patiently nearby with the reins already in position. Blondie was quite a bit taller than

Star, but not nearly as high as Zipper. Could she get on without help?

Megan grabbed hold of Blondie's thick mane. She bounced once or twice besides the pony and then sprang up along her side. All she managed to do was thump her knees into Blondie's ribs, causing the little pony to grunt, before landing back on her feet on the ground.

Megan tried again, this time springing higher into the air, but still she couldn't get onto Blondie's back. "You're too fat, Blondie," Megan grumbled. "And I can't get a good grip."

Blondie swished her tail and took a step forward. *I might be fat,* she seemed to say, *but you're banging me in the sides, and that isn't so great either!*

"I can dismount and give you a boost," Kendra offered.

"Let me try one more time," Megan said. She took a deep breath and bounced as high as she could beside the little Palomino. This time she managed to hook her elbows up on Blondie's back, but no matter how hard she struggled, she couldn't get up any higher.

Finally Megan landed back on her feet with a groan. "OK," she said. "Ruth-Ann said she needed stairs or an elevator to get on. Maybe that's what I should do."

"Where are you going to find an elevator?" Ruth-Ann asked.

"Watch," Megan said. She led Blondie over to the nearby arena fence. She positioned Blondie near the wooden rails and then scampered up the fence as though it was a ladder. In a moment she was on Blondie's golden back.

"Ahhh!" Megan sighed. "Maybe a fat pony isn't so bad, after all. Blondie's as comfortable as a big easy-chair!"

"Blondie isn't fat," Kendra said. "She's fluffy!"

"Blondie's fat and fluffy!" Megan said. "And she'd be a lot fatter if we didn't ride so often. But right now I'm kinda glad she's so chubby. She feels great bareback!"

Before long the girls were giggling and squealing as they rode the ponies around the ring. They didn't keep to a walk for long, but soon were bouncing at a trot and lope all around the riding arena. Once while Kendra was trotting she slid sideways and toppled off Star, landing on her feet. And several times Megan had to grab Blondie's long mane to keep herself from doing the same thing.

Only Ruth-Ann, who had been the most nervous to begin with, seemed to find trotting and loping easy. "Maybe it's easier for me because Zipper moves slower and isn't as bouncy as the smaller ponies," Ruth-Ann suggested.

"Maybe," Kendra agreed.

"I think Ruth-Ann can stay on because Zipper actually has a backbone and withers," Megan said. "Blondie and Star have such wide backs they're like sitting on barrels! They might be comfortable, but they're easy to tip off." She nudged Blondie with her heels and loped around the arena once again, coming to a halt to catch her breath.

"Try jumping!" Kendra suggested.

Megan looked at the jumps. "Are you trying to kill me?" she asked, laughing. "Blondie would make it over, but I'd fly off and land on my head!"

"You have a hard head!" Kendra said.

"Not that hard," Megan said.

"We aren't allowed to jump if Trish isn't here," Ruth-Ann reminded the others. "Remember?"

The girls couldn't help remembering Trish's recent lecture about jumping safety. So with a sigh they decided they would do something else before quitting for the day.

A Fourth "Ready to Ride" Girl

The Ready to Ride Club had just finished setting up three barrels in the barrel racing pattern when they saw a car turn down the Lewis driveway. The car drove past the house and barn and straight over to the riding arena. The girls halted their ponies.

"It's Mrs. Boris," Megan said. "She's the Russian lady who lives in the big house across the road."

A short, round lady climbed out from behind the steering wheel. She waved at the three girls cheerfully. "Hi, Mrs. Boris," Megan said politely. "If you're looking for my mom, I think she's at the house."

"I wasn't looking for your mother," Mrs. Boris said. "I was looking for you, Megan. And your lovely little horses."

A dark-haired girl about Megan's size slid out of the car and came over to the arena fence. She was dressed in an extra-large t-shirt and baggy blue jeans. Her narrow face was covered by a huge smile as she reached through the fence and patted Zipper, the nearest pony.

"Hello," the girl said. She seemed to be talking to the ponies as much as to the girls.

"This is Nadia," Mrs. Boris said. "She's from Belarus, and she's staying with me all summer."

Nadia nodded her head but didn't say anything else. Instead she scratched Zipper's curious nose, and then reached across to Star, who had wandered her direction to make certain she got attention too.

"Nadia has stayed with me for two weeks so far," Mrs. Boris continued. "And she's already very bored. I thought she would like to read, or go to the beach, or do crafts with me. But instead all she talks about is horses. Horses, horses, horses. Day after day she begs for us to stop and look at your horses. Today I said 'Yes.' "

Blondie seemed to finally notice that the other ponies were being petted, and she sidestepped over to Nadia. The dark-haired girl scratched Star's forehead one more time before rubbing Blondie's golden face.

"Hi, Nadia," Megan said. "I'm Megan. And this is my pony, Blondie."

Nadia stopped petting the ponies for a moment and looked up at Megan. "You have a nice yellow horse," she said. "Yellow horses are my best." Her voice was soft, and she had a thick accent. Megan had to concentrate to understand the girl.

Mrs. Boris began to speak rapidly. She told the R2R girls about Nadia. "She comes from Belarus, which is a small country near Russia," Mrs. Boris said. "Many years ago there was a nuclear accident in the Ukraine, and the wind blew that pollution to Belarus.

Because of the nuclear pollution, many Belarus children get cancer or other health problems. So every summer the children leave to stay at another country. That helps them be more healthy."

Megan looked at Nadia. She couldn't imagine leaving her family and friends and staying with total strangers for the whole summer.

"Nadia's parents live in the city, but her *babushka* and *dyehdushka*—her grandmother and grandfather—live in the country," Mrs. Boris continued. "Nadia goes there sometimes and rides their horse."

"I love horses," Nadia said. "My grandfather has a yellow horse like this, but he is bigger. Very big. Like an elephant, he's so big. But I don't get to ride him very much, because he has to work hard pulling a car."

"He pulls a car?" Kendra asked.

"Sorry," Nadia said. "My English isn't so good sometimes. Not a car, a . . ." She couldn't think of the word.

"Do you mean he pulls a cart?" Megan asked.

"Yes," Nadia said. "That's it. A cart."

"I just don't know what to do with Nadia," Mrs. Boris said. "I've taken her to the swimming pool, but she doesn't want to swim. I've taken her to the mall, but she doesn't like to shop. All she wants to do is ride horses."

"I could help take care of your horses," Nadia said. "Or I could clean the barn. I help my grandfather clean his barn all the time—I know how to do it very good."

"Our ponies don't live in the barn," Megan said. "So it isn't messy."

"I could clean your stuff," Nadia said. "I use a rag and soap to clean my grandfather's stuff."

"Stuff?"

"The things you sit on when you ride," Nadia said. "Those brown things. Except you aren't using them today, so maybe you don't need help cleaning them."

"Saddles," Ruth-Ann said. "We have saddles, but we aren't using them today."

"We're riding bareback for the fun of it today," Kendra said.

"Do you like to clean saddles and barns?" Megan asked.

"I would do anything to be with horses," Nadia said. "Especially your horses. They are so very beautiful. I would do anything if I could ride them sometimes."

Kendra, Ruth-Ann, and Megan looked at each other.

"Or if you don't want me to ride your horses, that is OK too," Nadia said. "I would be happy if I could even be near them sometimes."

"Do you know how to ride a pony?" Ruth-Ann asked.

Nadia shook her head. "Only a little," she said. "Not very good."

"Nadia could take lessons from Trish," Megan said. "She's coming tomorrow."

"Who would pay for her lessons?" Ruth-Ann asked.

"I could pay," Mrs. Boris said. "But does this lady have a nice horse for Nadia to borrow?"

"Trish doesn't bring her horses to our riding lessons," Kendra said.

"Then Nadia won't be able to ride with you," Mrs. Boris decided, "because she wouldn't have a horse to ride."

"She could ride Blondie," Megan said. "She's good with beginners."

"Blondie? But you're riding Blondie!" Kendra exclaimed.

Megan looked at Nadia, who was staring back at her with big, excited eyes. Megan suddenly realized that there were probably hundred of girls out there in the world who would like to ride but didn't have a pony as wonderful as Blondie. Megan couldn't help all of them, but maybe she could help this girl.

"If Blondie and I had our lesson first," Megan said thoughtfully, "then she could rest while you two go next. At the end, Nadia could have a lesson. Trish makes her beginning riders work at a walk most of the time, so it wouldn't be that difficult."

"Are you sure?" Kendra asked.

"Trish is a good teacher," Megan said. "She would keep Nadia and Blondie safe."

"Maybe your mom has another pony Nadia could borrow," Ruth-Ann suggested.

"Blondie is our only pony," Megan said. "And my mom's Morgans are all quite tall."

"Let's put away the ponies and phone Trish," Kendra suggested. They dismounted and turned to Mrs. Boris, who was standing by the car with a confused expression on her face.

"I should talk to your parents," Mrs. Boris said.

"My mom's at the house," Megan called over her shoulder. The four girls headed over to the hitching post, all chattering loudly. Nadia was the first one to grab a curry-comb. She began to brush the left side of Blondie while Megan brushed the right.

"We're going to have a sleep-over tonight," Megan said as they brushed and combed. "Right here at my barn."

"You have beds in your barn?" Nadia asked.

Kendra giggled. "We bring our sleeping bags and sleep on the bales in the hayloft," she said. "It's lots of fun. And we'll have a Ready to Ride meeting."

"Ready to Ride?" Nadia asked. She picked up a mane brush and began to carefully pick knots out of Blondie's long mane.

"It's a club," Ruth-Ann explained. "For kids who like horses. We have lots of fun."

"I like horses," Nadia said.

"Maybe you could be in our club," Megan said.

"Except she doesn't have a pony of her own," Kendra said.

"It isn't the 'Own Your Own Pony' Club," Ruth-Ann said. "It's the 'Ready to Ride' Club. And it sounds like Nadia's always ready to ride."

"Do you have a sleeping bag?" Megan asked.

"What is a sleeping bag?" Nadia asked.

Megan thought for a moment. "A sleeping bag is a big, thick blanket that zips together," she finally said. "You could use my sister's sleeping bag tonight, if you want."

"I will ask Mrs. Boris if she has one," Nadia said. "But I don't think so. We use regular blankets at her house."

"And we need to bring snacks," Kendra said. "Our parents normally don't let us eat junk food, but we're allowed to snack when we have our sleep-overs. They say it's a special treat."

"What food should I bring?" Nadia asked.

"Bring your favorite," Ruth-Ann said.

"OK," Nadia said.

"It gets kinda cold at night," Megan warned the girl.

"I'm used to the cold," Nadia said. "Sometimes in the winter we have no gas in our house. The whole city has no gas. All of Belarus has no gas. The people have to burn wood and garbage to try and keep warm.

Sometimes I have to sleep with my coat and pants and other clothes on."

"Wow!" The girls all stared at Nadia, but she didn't seem aware of them as she patiently untangled a big knot in Blondie's forelock.

After a few minutes, Megan stepped back and admired Blondie. Every hair on her mane and tail was perfect, thanks to Nadia's work with the brush.

Blondie seemed to enjoy having two girls work on her. She hung her head comfortably and rested one hind foot. She wasn't worried that there were more girls than ponies.

Megan didn't think she was worried, either. But she'd just have to wait and see how things went. Another girl for their Ready to Ride Club could be fun. Or it could be awful.

By tomorrow they'd know.

The Sleep-Over

The four girls pushed and pulled until they had rearranged the square hay bales into a longer-than-usual row. Then they covered the bales with a large blue tarp. "We need the tarp," Kendra explained to Nadia. "Otherwise the hay pokes right through the sleeping bags and keeps us awake."

"But the tarp is slippery," Megan warned. "So you have to be careful, or your sleeping bag will slide right off the bales in the middle of the night. Especially if you have a shiny sleeping bag."

"All sleeping bags are shiny," Ruth-Ann

said. "I wonder why." They positioned their sleeping bags and pillows in a row.

"Snack time!" Ruth-Ann said. "What did everyone bring to eat?"

Megan pulled a plate of cookies out of her backpack. "Cookies," she said. "I have three types. Oreo, chocolate chip, and ginger snaps. And the ginger snaps are homemade."

"Who's home?" Ruth-Ann asked.

"Who's home what?"

"Whose home made the homemade cookies?" Ruth-Ann said with a laugh.

"My home, of course," Megan said.

"I didn't know you could bake," Ruth-Ann said.

"I don't bake," Megan said. "But Mandy does."

"Your big sister gave you some of her cookies? Wow!"

"Two for each of us," Megan said.

"They look delicious," Ruth-Ann said. She picked up one and popped it into her mouth.

"Hey!" Megan said. "What did you bring?"

"Potato chips," Ruth-Ann said. "I have a

whole bag of sour cream and onion. And a few crumbs of my favorite type, ketchup."

"What happened to the rest?" Kendra asked. "Did you eat them before you got here?"

"Mikey," Ruth-Ann said.

"Your little brother!" The girls rolled their eyes.

"He found the bags at the bottom of my backpack," Ruth-Ann said. "I guess ketchup is Mikey's favorite too."

"Mikey will eat anything that doesn't eat him first!" Megan said.

"I brought us something to drink," Kendra announced. She pulled a large pitcher and four plastic glasses out of her pack. "I hope it didn't leak."

"Your dad's famous lemonade?" Megan asked.

"Better than that," Kendra said. "His world famous *pink cherry* lemonade. With ice cubes."

"At least it isn't black lemonade!" Megan laughed. They remembered the recent Fun Fair where Mr. Rawling accidentally added

The Sleep-Over

too much food coloring to his cotton candy and made it black.

"Dad made the ice cubes with frozen ginger ale," Kendra said. "They're very good."

"I wonder if Zipper would eat an ice cube?" Ruth-Ann said thoughtfully.

"Let's try," Kendra said.

"What did you bring to eat?" Megan asked, turning to Nadia, who had been sitting quietly off to the side.

"Mrs. Boris sent my best food," Nadia said.

"Fudge?" Ruth-Ann asked.

"Ice-cream?" Kendra asked.

"Popcorn?" Megan guessed.

"Even better than that," Nadia said. She held up a white plastic grocery bag. "Bananas," she said. "One for each of us."

"Bananas?" Megan asked. She looked in the bag and then back at Nadia.

"What type of bananas?" Ruth-Ann asked.

"Banana bananas," Megan said. She lifted up a cluster of four yellow bananas. "What other type is there?"

47

The girls didn't say anything, but they looked at Nadia and then the bananas again. They all liked fruit well enough, but it certainly wasn't a special treat for an exciting evening with the R2R Club.

"You not like bananas?" Nadia asked.

"They're OK," Kendra said.

"I'll have one later," Ruth-Ann said.

"I like bananas," Megan replied. She split a banana out of the bunch and pulled back the peel.

Nadia smiled shyly. "I love bananas best of all," she said. "Ten times best of all. Mrs. Boris buys me some every time she shops. In Belarus we never get any fruit to eat."

"Never?" Kendra asked.

"Never," Nadia repeated.

"Apples?" Megan said. "Or oranges?"

"Grapes?" Kendra said. "I love green grapes. And purple ones too."

"Or watermelon?" Ruth-Ann said.

"Watermelon?" Nadia asked. "What is that?"

"It's a fruit that's really big," Ruth-Ann

said, making a watermelon-sized circle with her hands. "It's green and hard on the outside. Red on the inside, and it has little black seeds. It's very juicy and tastes good."

"Ahr-booz," Nadia said.

"What?"

"Ahr-booz, that's watermelon," Nadia said. "We have none."

"Peaches or pears?" Megan asked.

"Nothing," Nadia said. "Except sometimes there are little wild apples that grow on the trees. They're OK. But not as good as bananas."

"Oh."

"Last year my mother bought me a banana," Nadia continued. "She put it in my stocking. I was so happy."

"You got a banana for a Christmas present?"

"Bananas and other fruit are much money," Nadia said. "We don't have much money."

Megan looked at the bananas with new respect. She ate fresh fruit all the time, sometimes several times a day. It was good, but it never seemed like anything very special. Maybe it would be if she didn't get it on a regular basis.

"I wonder if Zipper would eat a banana," Ruth-Ann said.

"You would give a banana to a horse?" Nadia asked.

"Just a little piece," Ruth-Ann said. The girls stood up with a giggle. They fished several ice cubes out of the lemonade and broke off a chunk of Megan's banana. Then Kendra turned on a flashlight, and the girls slipped down the ladder of the hayloft.

The three ponies were in a small corral near the barn. Zipper was already lying down in the center of the corral. When the girls arrived he lifted his head for a moment, and then with a groan flopped back over in the straw.

I can't play tonight, girls, he seemed to say. *I'm sleeping.*

Star and Blondie wandered over. They each tasted an ice cube but both wrinkled their noses and let the cube fall onto the ground, where it quickly melted.

Star sniffed the banana but turned her nose up at that as well.

Blondie wasn't so certain. She nuzzled the piece of banana, sniffing loudly. She put out her tongue and licked it, and then backed up a step. She seemed to think about the taste for a moment. Then she walked forward and licked the banana again.

Before long the little mare ate the whole piece of banana, and began to sniff and snort for more.

"Blondie is like me," Nadia says. "She likes bananas best too."

"I guess Zipper isn't the only pony that eats strange food!" Megan said with a laugh. She told Nadia about Zipper's taste in candies. "He loves red licorice," she said. "And gumdrops."

"But he doesn't like chocolate very much," Ruth-Ann said. They each gave the ponies a last pat and then hurried back up to the hayloft for their Ready to Ride meeting and sleep-over.

A New Riding Lesson

"This is Seeker," Megan told Nadia a few days later. "My mother suggested that you use her for your riding lesson with Trish."

Mrs. Lewis led the tall Palomino horse over to the hitching post and tied her near Blondie. "She's getting old now," Mrs. Lewis said, standing back to admire the mare. "But I think she'll be sound enough for your riding lessons."

"She is yellow just like Megan's horse," Nadia said. "My best color."

"Seeker is Blondie's mother," Megan explained. "She's a registered Morgan, and her real name is High Hills Goldseeker. Blondie's father was a Welsh pony named Mr. Good Luck Charm. When Blondie was born my mom took the 'Gold' out of Seeker's name, and the 'Good' out of the sire's name to come up with 'Good as Gold Blondie.'"

"That is how we name people in Belarus!" Nadia said.

"You take your mom and dad's names to make a new name?" Megan asked.

"Let me say it right," Nadia said. "Mrs. Boris's real name is Mrs. Borisovna, but she says that's too hard for you to talk. Her father's first name was Boris. When he had a baby girl, they put 'ovna' on to make her last name. If Boris had a baby boy, his last name would be Borisovich."

"That's confusing," Ruth-Ann said, scratching her head.

"Not as hard as a name like High Hills Goldseeker," Nadia said. "There are no high hills on Seeker. Why would they name her that?"

"High Hills is the name of the stable where Seeker was born," Mrs. Lewis said.

"They name horses after barns?" Nadia asked. "That's even badder than naming them after their father."

Everyone laughed.

The four girls had their animals saddled and ready when Trish arrived for lessons. Megan introduced Nadia to Trish.

"Could Nadia ride first?" Megan asked. "Mrs. Boris needs to take her to the eye doctor after dinner."

"Mrs. Boris takes very good care of me," Nadia said. "But I would rather be with horses than go to the doctor."

"I'll be glad to do Nadia's lesson first," Trish said. "But we will need to unsaddle Seeker."

"Unsaddle?"

"I want to start Nadia properly," Trish said. "And that means that she needs to learn the correct way to saddle and bridle a horse. Ground work is just an important as riding. In fact, it's probably more important. If you can't prepare a horse to ride, you can't ride."

Nadia had a difficult time saddling and bridling Seeker. The Morgan mare was much taller than the ponies, and Nadia wasn't a very big ten-year-old. But Seeker stood quietly as Nadia struggled to get everything into position.

Learning to mount was also a bit more difficult than usual. Trish ended up pulling a square straw bale into the ring and using it for a mounting block. "There is nothing wrong with standing on something when you mount," Trish said. "In fact, it can hurt your horse's back if you have to pull hard to get on."

Trish started by showing Nadia the proper way to hold the reins. She explained the cues used to move a horse from a halt to a walk, and then how to stop it again. She explained how to turn a horse to the left and right.

Seeker was quiet and obedient. And she didn't get excited when Nadia accidentally dropped one rein, and it trailed in the sand besides her until Trish walked over and picked up the rein.

At the end of the lesson Nadia chatted happily about how much fun she'd had. "Seeker is very good horse," Nadia said. "Maybe we should give her some banana for a bite."

Trish looked curiously at the girl.

The R2R girls giggled, and explained how Blondie had discovered bananas earlier in the week. "But we don't know if Seeker likes bananas," Ruth-Ann said. "Maybe she has different tastes than her daughter."

"Maybe Seeker says *ahr-booz* best," Nadia said.

"What?" Now Trish looked even more confused.

"That's Russian for watermelon," Megan explained.

"I'm glad you enjoyed your lesson, Nadia," Trish said. "You were a perfect student. You paid attention and followed all my instructions."

"Will I ride Seeker next week?" Nadia asked. She reached as high as she could to brush the Palomino's back.

"My mom said you can use Seeker anytime you want," Megan said.

"There is one problem with Seeker," Trish said.

"She's too tall?" Kendra asked, patting her own small pony.

"Yes, Seeker's too tall for Nadia," Trish said. "But that's not the real problem."

"Then what's wrong?" Ruth-Ann asked.

"Seeker behaved very well today," Trish said. "That's why older horses make excellent mounts for beginners. But Seeker moves a bit stiffly, even at a walk. I suspect she has the beginnings of arthritis."

"She's almost twenty-eight years old," Mrs. Lewis said, coming around the corner just in time to catch the last of the conversation.

"She's getting up there in years," Trish said.

"Morgans develop slower than many other breeds," Mrs. Lewis said. "But they also live longer than a lot of other horses. I know some Morgans that are more than thirty years old."

"That's true," Trish said. "But Nadia is doing so well I expect she'll be trotting by the end of next week. And I don't think it would be fair to expect Seeker to trot very much."

"And Nadia needs a horse that she can ride with us between lessons," Megan said. "We have lots of fun riding all week long, not just on lesson days."

"I don't think Nadia should ride any horse this week unless an adult is present," Trish said. "She won't have the necessary skills to help herself if she ever had a big problem."

"We'll help her," Ruth-Ann said.

"And Seeker isn't going to give her any problems," Megan said.

"Maybe not," Trish said. "But strange things can happen."

"Like what?" Kendra asked.

"Well," Trish said, "what if something loud scares Seeker?"

"Such as?"

"A gun shot or a car backfiring," Trish replied.

"No one is going to shoot near our house," Megan said. "And I've never heard a car backfire. Why should it happen now?"

"My father always said 'expect the unexpected,' " Trish replied. "Those sorts of things can happen. Or suppose you girls were riding your ponies near some trees, and someone bumped a hornet's nest. What do you think your ponies would do?"

"Run!" Megan said.

"Buck!" Ruth-Ann said.

"Kick," Kendra said.

"That's probably right," Trish agreed. "And what would you do then?"

"If Zipper bucked I'd probably fall off," Ruth-Ann said.

Trish laughed. "Probably," she said. "But if you didn't fall off, what would you do to get control of your pony?"

"Pull on one rein?" Ruth-Ann answered.

"Turn them sharply," Kendra said. "They can't run away if they're turning."

"That's right," Trish said. "But until Nadia has had more experience, she won't know to do these things. So I don't think she should ride alone for a while."

Nadia's face must have shown her disappointment, because Trish looked at her with a smile. "Don't worry, Nadia," she said. "Before long you'll be able to ride with the other girls. And for now you can spend time doing ground work with Seeker and the ponies. You should come over often and practicing leading them. Lead them all around the ring, and over the poles and bridge. Saddle and unsaddle one of the ponies at first—maybe Blondie or Star—since they'll be easier to reach. There are lots of things you can do until our next lesson."

"I will be happy," Nadia said. "Thank you."

Mrs. Boris drove up in a cloud of dust. "Time to go, Nadia," she called. "Your appointment is in half an hour."

Nadia groaned. "I hope I don't need glasses," she said. "And the next day I must go to the dentist. That will be even badder."

She gave Seeker's shoulder one last scratch and turned to climb into the car.

"Did you have fun?" Mrs. Boris asked the girl.

"I had a very good time," Nadia said. "Good, good, ten times ten good."

"How much money do I owe you?" Mrs. Boris asked Trish.

Trish shook her head. "Nothing," she said.

"Nothing?"

"I would be happy to give Nadia riding lessons while she is here this month," Trish said. "I'm coming to the Lewises' place to work with the other girls anyhow. So it's really no extra work."

"Are you certain?" Mrs. Boris asked.

"I'm certain," Trish replied.

When Mrs. Boris and Nadia were gone, the other girls turned to Trish. "You're going to give Nadia free riding lessons?" Ruth-Ann asked.

"Yes," Trish said. "I'm going to give her free lessons."

"Why?"

"Do you know that Mrs. Boris raised more than two thousand dollars to bring Nadia here from Belarus?" Trish asked. "And now that Nadia's here, Mrs. Boris is paying for her food and clothing. Riding lessons are something I can do for them. In fact, it's something I can do to serve God."

"I can see that you'd be serving Nadia and Mrs. Boris by giving them free lessons," Megan said. "But how is a free riding lesson serving God?"

"There's a place in the Bible where Jesus says if you give someone a drink of cold water, or clothes to wear, you're actually serving God," Trish said. "I might not be giving Nadia something to eat or drink, but I am doing something that's very important to her."

"I guess you're right," Megan said thoughtfully. "I hadn't looked at it that way."

Nadia Keeps Riding

Nadia came over almost every day and worked with Seeker and the ponies. She practiced saddling and bridling. She led the ponies around the ring, making them stop and start when she wanted. Mrs. Lewis even taught the girl how to lunge Seeker in a circle around her. Before long Nadia could make Seeker walk, trot, and halt on her command.

"Trish was right," Mrs. Lewis said, shaking her head as she watched one day. "Seeker does have a slight limp when she trots."

When Trish came the following week, she was impressed to see how confidently

Nadia saddled and bridled Seeker. Then the girl mounted and dismounted easily, although she still had to use the bale to get on the tall horse. And before long she was walking Seeker through various patterns, first zigzagging around pylons, and later making the mare step over ground poles.

At the end of the lesson Trish came over to the group and praised them for all their help with Nadia's ground work. "But there's still one problem," Trish said.

"Did we do something wrong?" Ruth-Ann asked, mounting Zipper.

"Yes," Trish said. "You did too good of a job. Nadia is ready to trot, and Seeker isn't going to be suitable for that."

"Trish, Nadia can ride Blondie," Megan said. "I really don't mind. Except the four of us will have to share three ponies, and that won't be as much fun."

"I have a suggestion," Trish said.

"We're listening," Kendra said.

"I think Nadia can safely ride Seeker with you this week," Trish said. "*If* she stays in the riding arena and only walks. Plus, she must wear a helmet all the time. OK?"

Nadia grinned widely.

"And," Trish continued, "I think she can do some of her riding lesson on Seeker next week too. But maybe she could use Blondie during the last part of her lessons, when it's time for her to learn how to trot."

"Won't it be hard for Nadia to take lessons on both Seeker and Blondie?" Kendra asked. "I'm really used to my own pony, but I feel strange when I ride Blondie or Zipper."

"Nadia doesn't have her own pony in Belarus," Trish said. "It will be good for her to practice on different horses here, and then she can handle different ones there."

Megan was startled for a moment. She had almost forgotten that Nadia would be returning to Belarus soon. "I'll be glad to share Blondie with Nadia," Megan said.

"I'm proud of you," Trish said. "Sharing Blondie with Nadia is a kind thing to do. And I think God's proud of you too."

"God?" Nadia asked.

Megan wondered how to explain God. Finally she got an idea. She folded her hands and bowed her head. "God," she said.

"Oh," Nadia said. *"Bohkh.* I not know *Bohkh.* He not speak Russian, I think."

"God speaks all languages," Trish said. "And He loves you, Nadia. Even if you don't know Him yet."

"Maybe," Nadia said. "Thank you, Megan. I am most lucky. Two yellow horses to ride. And I am always ready to ride, just like your club!"

Horse Show Plans

When Trish arrived for riding lessons the following week, the girls met her at the arena with the Hastings Lake Horse Show booklet in their hands.

"We need help," Kendra said. "We don't know which classes to enter."

"I think this book's written in Russian," Ruth-Ann moaned. "Or Chinese. We don't even know what it's saying half the time."

"That book not Russian!" Nadia said. "I know Russian."

"What are you talking about?" Trish said, peering at the booklet over Ruth-Ann's shoulder.

"What's this mean?" Kendra said. "What's a 'green hunter'? Or 'maiden English pleasure'?"

Trish chuckled. "Horse talk is rather complicated," she agreed. "Both *green* and *maiden* are words that mean a horse that's just beginning to learn something. Horses can't enter those classes if they've won a lot of ribbons before." She flipped through the book quickly. "Let's take a few minutes and choose which classes you'll enter. Then we'll get on to riding lessons."

Everyone sat down on the grass near Trish. "Western classes are first at this show," Trish said. "You'll be in the ten-and-under age group. There are two different Western classes you can enter. Western equitation is judged on the rider—how smoothly you ride and control your horse. And the second class is Western pleasure, which is judged on the horse, how prettily it moves and behaves at a walk, slow jog, and lope."

"I want to enter both those classes," Ruth-

Ann said. "Zipper is slow, so maybe we'll do well at Western."

Kendra said she also wanted to enter both Western classes, but Megan shook her head. "Blondie and I don't do very well in Western," Megan said. "She jogs too fast, and she's a bit rough. We aren't allowed to post when we show Western, so I bounce when Blondie jogs. And Blondie passes all the other horses, and the judge doesn't like that in pleasure. Western horses are supposed to be slow."

"That's fine," Trish said. "You still have two English classes you can enter, but this time the youngest class is for children ages thirteen and under. That may make English classes a bit more difficult." All three girls decided they would enter English pleasure and English equitation with their ponies.

"We won't be jealous if the other girls win," Ruth-Ann said.

"That's good," Trish said. "Because you know that I believe ribbons aren't nearly as important as people."

"We know," Megan said.

"God doesn't care about ribbons either," Trish said. "He cares about people."

Megan, Kendra, and Ruth-Ann all nodded their heads. Nadia listened but didn't say anything.

Trish explained the different jumping classes. 'Hunter' classes were judged on the horse's style of jumping, and 'jumper' classes were judged on their speed and ability.

Ruth-Ann said Zipper wouldn't enter any hunter or jumper classes. But after her four regular riding classes they would enter a game called The Dollar Game. Trish explained that everyone would ride bareback in this class and sit on a dollar bill. They would walk, trot, and canter, and the winner would be the last person with the paper still underneath them!

"Do we keep the money?" Ruth-Ann asked.

"The winner gets everyone's money," Trish said.

"Ruth-Ann is an expert bareback rider!" Kendra said, laughing. "She's certain to win."

"Don't be so certain," Trish said. "This class is open to older kids, and even adults, so there will be a lot of very good riders. But it will be fun, and that's the most important thing."

Kendra was entering the same four riding classes as Ruth-Ann. She would also enter thirteen-and-under hunter hack. "It will be a good way to start Star jumping," Trish said. "It will have only two low jumps, and she won't have to rush and hurry."

Megan wasn't going to ride Western, but she would enter English pleasure and English equitation. Then she would enter the open youth jumper class.

"The jumps could be as high as two and a half feet," Trish said. "And any rider under the age of sixteen can enter. But I think you'll do fine, since Blondie is easily jumping that height now."

71

When the girls were all finished with their entries, they turned and looked at Nadia, who was now busy scratching the ponies.

Trish looked at Nadia and then at Megan. She raised her eyebrows but didn't say anything.

Megan looked at Trish. *I wonder if she's thinking what I'm thinking.*

"Maybe Nadia . . ." Megan began.

"Would she be ready to show . . ." Kendra asked slowly.

"Walk/trot classes could be a lot of fun," Ruth-Ann said.

This time Trish seemed to know where they were going. "Nadia," she said. "Have you ever thought about going to the Hastings Lake horse show?"

"Why, yes!" Nadia said. "I will come and watch. I can help you get the horses ready. I can brush them good."

"But would you like to ride in the walk/trot class at the show?" Megan said.

"Seeker can't trot," Nadia said. "It would hurt her legs."

"Maybe you could ride Blondie in the walk/trot class," Megan said. "Look. It says you can go either English or Western in walk/trot. And it's after my classes, so we can easily share Blondie."

Nadia stared at Megan, and then turned to Trish. "I could ride at horse show?" she asked. "A real horse show?"

"I believe you and Blondie would do very well at walk/trot," Trish said.

"Do you want to enter?" Megan asked.

"Yes!" Nadia said. "Yes! Yes! Yes! A thousand million ten times yes!"

Trish reached down and ruffled Nadia's dark hair. "OK," she said. "We all have a lot of work to do. Hurry and get your ponies. We need to practice show ring protocol. We have only two weeks before the show."

The four girls spent the next hour working together in the riding ring. Nadia rode Seeker and kept the mare at a walk, while the other girls worked at all three gaits.

"Safety is the most important thing to remember," Trish explained. "You must keep at least one horse length between you and the other horses. Two horse-lengths are even better."

"What is horse length?" Nadia asked, wrinkling her forehead.

"A horse length is a space that is as long as a horse," Trish said. "If you get closer, you could easily be kicked by that horse."

Trish showed them how to safely pass another pony. "You must always pass on the inside," Trish said. "Never try to fit between another horse and the rail. It would be very easy to get squished there. And when you pass, you must be careful that you don't cut anyone off."

"Cut anyone off?" Nadia said. "How would I cut someone?"

Trish laughed. "Not cut them with something sharp," she said. "Cut them off means you get in their way. They have to stop or else they'd run into you. You need to have very good manners when you show."

At the end of the group lesson, Megan dismounted and watched as Nadia practiced trotting Blondie. Two weeks earlier, Nadia's legs had flopped back and forth when she trotted, but lately she had become very smooth. All Nadia's practice was making a big difference. Nadia now posted up and down comfortably to Blondie's extended trot.

Megan hoped Nadia and Blondie would do well at the show. It might be the only horse show Nadia would ever ride in.

And in a few weeks she would be going home. And maybe she would never be back.

The Hastings Lake Horse Show

The morning of the horse show dawned cool and cloudy. Everyone kept glancing at the sky as they hurried with their last preparations.

"I hope it doesn't rain," Kendra moaned, looking at her white pony. "It was hard cleaning Star. Mud would ruin everything."

"I will help you keep Star clean," Nadia said. "I have big time to help."

Mrs. Lewis sighed. "Sometimes they cancel horse shows when it rains," she said. "My Morgan show at Calgary was canceled this spring due to bad weather."

"Cancel?" Nadia asked. "What is to cancel?"

"It means to stop something," Trish said.

"Stop!" Nadia exclaimed. "I don't want the show to stop."

The three mothers and Mrs. Boris looked at each other and frowned. The Ready to Ride Club members frowned too.

"Well," Trish said. "Then we should pray for nice weather, and leave the rest up to God. OK?"

Everyone bowed their head while Trish said a prayer. "Dear Jesus," Trish prayed out loud. "We want to thank you for the chance to enter a horse show with our friends. We know You are in control of everything, including the weather. If it's Your will, we ask that the weather gets better today. Please don't let the horse show be canceled. But if it does, help us to realize that You have a plan for everything, and that Your plans are better than ours. Amen."

"Thank you for the prayer, Trish," Mrs. Rawling said. "Now, I'm going to park my car near the bleachers. Would you ladies like to come sit inside with me? It will be warmer there, and we should be able to see clearly." The women all hurried after Kendra's mother.

"In Russia and Belarus no one prays," Nadia said. She straightened the collar of the English riding jacket she had borrowed. "There used to be a law—no praying. No going to church."

"Wow!" Kendra said. "It's against the law to go to church?"

"Not anymore," Nadia said. "But my parents never go to church. Not one time. My dad says God is pretend."

"God isn't pretend," Trish said. "Look at all the beautiful things in this world. There must have been an amazing Creator who could make horses and ponies and people and everything else. They couldn't have been made by a big accident."

"My doctor said that a person's heart and lungs and eyes are all miracles," Megan said. "God knew how to put them together so they would work perfectly."

"My heart works," Nadia said. "It is banging hard now. Very hard. Like a clock."

"Don't be nervous, Nadia," Megan said. "Blondie will behave well for you."

"I hope," Nadia said.

A loudspeaker crackled overhead. "First class of the morning begins in fifteen minutes," the announcer called. "Western pleasure ten-and-under. Please enter the hitching ring."

"That's us!" Kendra and Ruth-Ann squealed. They spun around, quickly pulling on cowboy hats and making certain their numbers were pinned securely on their backs before mounting Star and Zipper.

The weather remained cool, but it didn't rain during any of the Western classes. As Megan, Nadia, and Trish watched from the rail, Ruth-Ann and Zipper placed second in Western pleasure, and Kendra and Star placed third.

Next came various Western pleasure classes for older children and adults. When they were finished, ten-and-under Western equitation was called into the ring. This time Kendra placed second and Ruth-Ann placed third.

During a short break, everyone changed their horses out of Western tack and into English equipment. A few cool drops of rain fell, and then the rain paused.

When it was time for the thirteen-and-under English classes, Megan felt almost sick with nervousness. *God,* she prayed to herself as she entered the ring on Blondie, *please help me have a good attitude. Help me be happy if I don't win any ribbons. But please, help Blondie and I do our best, too.* She tried to smile at Kendra and Ruth-Ann as they entered the ring with her, but somehow her lips seemed stuck to her teeth.

The English pleasure class had eight pairs of horse and riders. The class seemed to pass in a blur as the announcer called out the different gaits. First they walked around the ring several times, and then they trotted. Megan concentrated on keeping Blondie's trot brisk but under control. Before long they were instructed to return to a walk.

"Canter, please," the loudspeaker then crackled. "Canter."

Megan moved her outside foot back and cued Blondie for the proper lead. The little mare took one step at a trot and then cantered off properly. Blondie was moving smoothly and paying careful attention to Megan as they once again returned to walk, and then changed directions to walk, trot, and canter the opposite way.

When the winners were announced, Megan and Blondie won first place. Kendra and Star were third, and Ruth-Ann and Zipper were fifth.

Ruth-Ann was grinning as she left the ring. "I know Zipper isn't a very good English horse," she said happily. "Because he likes to move so slowly, and English horses aren't supposed to be slow. But we did our best."

"I thought Zipper did a great job," Kendra said. "And Blondie was super, Megan. Congratulations!"

"Thanks," Megan said. She admired the bright first place ribbon.

"You looked excellent, honey!" Mrs. Lewis said. She was wearing a rain coat as she fed Blondie a horse treat. "That's your very first English class, and you brought home a first place ribbon!"

Nadia offered to pick out Blondie's hooves before the next class. She had barely finished when thirteen-and-under English equitation was called.

The English equitation class started smoothly, but when the group reversed to work the second direction of the ring, it began to rain. Blondie didn't want to turn her face into the wind and raindrops, and kept trying to swing her hips sideways, making it difficult for Megan to keep her moving the proper direction. Once, when she had a moment, Megan glanced up and saw that the other riders were having the same problem with their ponies. *Equitation is judged on the rider, anyhow,* Megan told herself. *So I just need to remain calm and do my best.*

When the ribbons were passed out, Megan and Blondie placed first again! This time Kendra and Star placed second, and Ruth-Ann and Zipper placed third. It was a clean sweep for the R2R Club!

Trish congratulated the group on a job well done. "It's very difficult to ride a horse in the rain," she said. "Look at the adults now, and you'll see they're having the same problems." One tall bay horse was even rearing in the ring.

"Would you like to put on your raincoat?" Mrs. Lewis asked. She passed a yellow slicker to Megan, who dismounted and carefully slid it over her outfit.

"Thanks, Mom," Megan said. She glanced at her borrowed English saddle and wondered if she could cover it with something so it was protected from the rain.

"With your two first place ribbons you'll be in the running for High Point English

13-and-under Rider," Mrs. Lewis said. She smiled at Megan. "I'm really proud of you. Hopefully your jumping class will go well too."

"Thanks," Megan said. But suddenly she felt even more nervous than usual. High Point English Rider! That would be amazing!

"Normally Blondie doesn't do such a good job," Mrs. Lewis continued.

"She's a better English horse than Western," Megan said. "And we've done a lot of work with Trish this summer."

"I'm really glad Mrs. Rawling found such a good trainer," Mrs. Lewis said.

Before long the rain stopped. The girls loosened their ponies' cinches but didn't unsaddle since they all had one last class before the day was finished. Nadia helped everyone dry off the top of their saddles, and then she ran back and forth fetching combs for the riders and brushes for the ponies' wet manes.

Trish was finished fixing Ruth-Ann's hair when the loudspeaker blared overhead.

"Attention, please," the announcer said. "Due to the unsettled weather we are going to open two rings for our last few classes. This way we hope to finish before the rain settles in again. Please pay attention so you know which ring your class will be in. There will be a five-minute break before we resume."

"Resume?" Nadia asked. "What is resume?"

"It means to start something again," Trish said.

"NahcheeNAHT!" Nadia said. "That's Russian for 'start.' We start soon."

"They're going to have two rings?" Kendra asked.

"They must have a second judge to help them," Trish said. "It will really speed things up."

"All the jumper and hunter classes will be in Ring A," the announcer said. "The walk/trot and games classes will be in Ring B."

"I'll be in Ring A," Megan said.

"Me too," Kendra added.

"The first class in Ring A will be the open youth jumping class," the announcer said. "Please have all those contestants meet at the A hitching ring now."

"That's me," Megan said. "And Blondie." She quickly tightened Blondie's cinch and slipped off her raincoat.

"We'll cheer for you!" Ruth-Ann called.

"In Ring B the first class will be youth walk/trot," the announcer continued. "Will all those riders please enter the B hitching ring."

"That's me!" Nadia squealed. "I'm in Ring B. Right?" She grabbed her riding helmet and slid it onto her head, doing up the buckle firmly.

Two Classes

Megan looked at Blondie.

Then she looked at Trish. The woman's face showed shock and worry and sadness all at once. Megan knew then that she had heard the announcer correctly.

Her jumping class was about to begin. And Nadia's walk/trot class was going to start at exactly the same time, but in a different ring.

Blondie couldn't be in two places at once. She could not jump with Megan and walk/trot for Nadia at the same time. Someone would have to miss their class.

Nadia wasn't aware of the problem. At least, not yet. Her poor English had probably made her miss the announcement's meaning. Instead her thin face beamed as she checked to make certain her jacket buttons were done up properly. "Is my number on?" she asked excitedly. "Do I look good?"

"You look great," Kendra said.

"I am so scared," Nadia said. "Scared. Scared. One hundred million times scared."

The Ready to Ride girls looked at each other and then back at Trish.

For once Trish didn't say anything.

You can win High Point English Rider if you do well in your jumping class, a voice seemed to say in Megan's head. *You've never been High Point Rider before. You've worked so hard for this all summer. Blondie is such a good jumper. And your mother will be so proud of you when you win.*

A different voice seemed to talk in Megan's other ear. *Nadia's going back to Belarus next week. She may never get to enter a horse show again. This is her only class. And she's worked hard with Blondie too.*

"Last call for youth open jumper," the loudspeaker called. "Please come to the A hitching ring."

Megan didn't have time to pray. Or to think. Instead she took a deep breath and picked up Blondie's reins.

Megan slipped the English reins over the little Palomino's neck. Then she turned to Nadia. "Let me give you a hand up," she said.

She helped Nadia slide into the saddle and pointed her toward Ring B. "You'll do well," she said.

"I hope," Nadia said. She clicked her tongue and walked Blondie forward. Then she halted and turned to Trish. "Is it OK if I pray to God? Not to win, but to be not so scared?"

Trish nodded. "We'll pray for you too," she said.

In a moment Nadia and Blondie were in the ring and circling with the other young riders. Trish slipped beside Megan and put an arm around her shoulders.

The walk/trot class went very smoothly. Blondie worked well for Nadia, circling the ring smoothly at her extended English trot, and then returning easily to a walk. When the class was finished and the ribbons were passed out, Nadia received a third place. She returned from the ring with a smile pasted from one side of her face to the other.

"I said a pray," Nadia said. "And I was not so afraid. It worked."

"God can speak Russian as well as He can speak English," Trish said. "I'm sure He heard every word you said, Nadia."

"Maybe," Nadia said. "I will take my ribbon home and show my mother and father. They will be so happy."

Mrs. Boris hurried over and hugged Nadia. Megan turned away and watched as the last rider on a small black horse finished the youth jumper class. The black horse hit one pole and then was eliminated because it wouldn't go over a jump.

Blondie wouldn't have refused, Megan thought. *And I doubt she'd have hit any jumps, either.*

The ribbons were passed out, and Megan

sighed. There had been some good horses in the class, but none were better than Blondie.

"We might have won," Megan said softly.

"You won already," Trish said.

Megan turned to the woman with a weak smile. "I'm glad Nadia rode in her walk/trot class," she said. "I know it was the right thing to do. But I still feel bad that I didn't get to enter my jumping class." Tears sprang to her eyes for a moment, and she blinked hard so they wouldn't spill down her face. "Why do I feel bad if I did the right thing?"

"Megan," Trish said, "doing the right thing can be really difficult. But remember, God isn't interested in ribbons and trophies and prizes. He's interested in our characters. He wants to know how we'll treat other people, and how we'll behave when we have problems. And today, Megan, you did something more important than winning another ribbon."

Megan slowly nodded her head. "And Nadia prayed," she said. "That was amazing too."

"Your pony did an excellent job for you both today," Trish said. "And you'll have many other good shows with Blondie in the future. She's going to be a top jumping horse."

"Yes," Megan said. "She was good as gold. Good as Gold Blondie."

Trish grinned and ruffled Megan's thick blond hair. "I know someone else who fits that name today," she said. "You! Today there were two 'Good as Gold Blondies'!"

"Thanks," Megan said.

"Now," Trish said. "We'd better see what Nadia is doing with your pony. I heard her ask Mrs. Boris for a banana. A thousand ten bananas, I think! So we'd better rescue Blondie before she eats so many bananas she turns yellow!"

"Yellow-er!" Megan said. "Because my pony's already gold, Trish. Blondie's good as gold."

Words of Advice on Getting a First Pony

I ride both English and Western, and my tack shed is stacked high with equipment. But what do you *need* when you first get a pony? There are entire stores filled to the brim with tack, but there are only a few items that you *must* have:

1. A saddle, either Western or English, that fits both you and your pony properly.

2. A bridle with reins and the type of bit that your pony works well in.

3. A saddle blanket or pad that fits the type of saddle you're using. It doesn't need to be fancy, but it must be able to protect your pony's back.

4. A sturdy halter with a strong lead rope. It must be strong enough that it won't break if your pony ever pulls back when he's tied.

5. A plastic currycomb, a soft body brush, and a hoof pick. In fact, you should have several hoof picks because they're easy to lose.

6. A certified riding helmet that fits your head properly.

7. A pair of riding boots of any style that has a heel so your feet don't slide through the stirrups, and so your toes have some protection if your pony accidentally steps on them!

8. A good attitude.

You can buy a saddle, bridle, blanket, halter, helmet, and riding boots at almost any tack store. You cannot buy a good attitude.

A good attitude comes from God (and your parents and friends can influence you too). Pray that God works with you as you work with your pony. I can totally guarantee that if you ride long enough, you're going to experience your share of horse problems.

If your pony misbehaves, you're going to be frightened. What do you do with your fear? Ignore it? Quit riding? Ask for help?

What will you do when you lose your patience? Your horse may step on your toe or embarrass you in front of your friends. Do you hit your pony? Sell him? Put him away?

There will be times when your pony disappoints you. You've worked hard to prepare for a horse show, and now he's lame. Maybe all your work seems like nothing but a waste of time. Maybe you wonder if you should even have a pony.

What are you going to do when you're disappointed or angry or afraid?

I suggest that if you ask God to help you with your attitude, you'll be able to deal in a positive manner with all these problems. Sometimes God will direct a person (such as someone like Trish) to help you. Sometimes He'll show you a better way to do things. And sometimes He'll show you that the problem comes from *you,* and *not* something or someone else!

Happy trails,
Heather Grovet

Want more horse stories? You'll enjoy these also.

The Sonrise Farm Series

Based on true stories, *Katy Pistole's* Sonrise Farm series about Jenny Thomas and her Palomino mare, Sunny, teaches children about horses and God's redeeming grace. (ages 11–13) Paperback, 128 pages each. US$7.99 each.

Book 1 **The Palomino**
Jenny Thomas has her heart set on one thing—a golden Palomino all her own. Her daring rescue of an abused horse at an auction begins an enduring friendship with Sunny. 0-8163-1863-8

Book 2 **Stolen Gold**
Book two in the series finds Sunny in the clutches of an abusive former owner who wants to collect insurance money on the Palomino and her colt. 0-8163-1882-4

Book 3 **Flying High**
A record-breaking jump, Sunny's reputation, and Jenny's relationship with God are all at stake when Jenny and her Palomino champion come face to face with their old enemy. 0-8163-1942-1

Book 4 **Morning Glory**
Sunny's foal is born, but an evil plan from Jenny's old enemy, Vanessa DuBois, threatens all of them. But God has a plan to restore their lives. 0-8163-2036-5

Order from your ABC by calling **1-800-765-6955**, or get online and shop our virtual store at **http://www.Adventist BookCenter.com**.
- Read a chapter from your favorite book
- Order online
- Sign up for e-mail notices on new products

Prices subject to change without notice.